Big Dog and Little Dog
Making a Mistake

Dav Pilkey

Houghton Mifflin Harcourt
Boston New York

For information about permission to reproduce selections from this book,
write to Permissions, Houghton Mifflin Harcourt Publishing Company,
215 Park Avenue South, New York, New York 10003.

Green Light Readers ® and its logo are trademarks of HMH Publishers LLC,
registered in the United States and other countries.

www.hmhco.com

Library of Congress Cataloging-in-Publication Data is on file.
ISBN: 978-0-544-65114-2 paper over board
ISBN: 978-0-544-65122-7 paperback

Manufactured in China
SCP 10 9 8 7 6 5 4 3 2 1
4500575152

Ages	Grades	Guided Reading Level	Reading Recovery Level	Lexile® Level
4–7	K	D	5–6	50L

For Samantha Jeanne Wills

Big Dog is going for a walk.

Little Dog is going, too.

Big Dog and Little Dog
see something.

What do they see?

Big Dog thinks it is a kitty.

Little Dog thinks so, too.

Sssssssssss.

But it does not *smell* like a kitty.

Big Dog smells bad.

Little Dog smells bad, too.

Big Dog and Little Dog

had a bad day.

They are going home now . . .

. . . just in time for a party!

<img_1 alt="paw print" /> Story Sequencing <img_1 alt="paw print" />

The story of Big Dog and Little Dog's mistake got scrambled! Can you put the scenes in the right order?

A

C

B

D

E

❧ On the Run! ❧

Is that a kitty? Use your finger to trace
the best path through the maze for
Big Dog and Little Dog to reach it.

🐾 Word Scramble 🐾

These words from the story got mixed up! Can you unscramble them and point to the correct words in th word box? Try writing a new story with these words

Word Box

ESE

TYPRA

MEHO

DAB

LELMS

KALW

TYKIT

PARTY

SMELL

BAD

WALK

KITTY

HOME

SEE

🐾 Bow-Wow! 🐾

Check out these amazing dog facts.

🐾 A German shepherd named Orient guided the first blind man to hike the entire Appalachian Trail—2,100 miles!

🐾 Norwegian lundehunds have six toes on each paw so they can climb steep cliffs and their ears fold down and seal shut to keep out dirt.

🐾 Dogs and people have many of the same organs, but dogs do not have appendixes.

🐾 Almost all dogs have pink tongues except for the chow chow and the shar-pei. Their tongues are black!

🐾 Dalmatian puppies' fur is completely white when they are born and their spots appear later.

🐾 Fill-in-the-Blank 🐾

Use the pictures to choose the missing word from the word box!

Word Box

smell
home
kitty
bad
walk
party

Big Dog and Little Dog are going for a ___ 🐾 ___ .

Big Dog and Little Dog think they see a ___ 🐾 ___ .

The kitty does not ___ 🐾 ___ like a kitty.

Big Dog and Little Dog smell .

Big Dog and Little Dog go .

They are just in time for the !